CORAL TRAIL

Sue Vyner

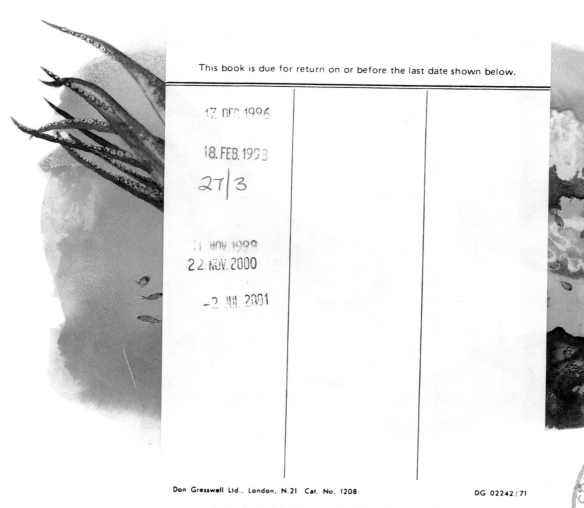

illustrated by
Tim Vyner

GOLLANCZ CHILDREN'S PAPERBACKS · LONDON

Down in the sea, the octopus is going back to her den.
But as she swims by the coral reef, something is following her.
A shoal of gleaming fish darts past.

"Swim faster! Something's coming," the octopus says to them.
"But as long as we stay together, there's far too many of us to catch,"
they tell her, and keep on swimming.

The octopus swims away.

A graceful sting-ray glides by. "Hide quickly!"
the octopus says. "There's something coming after us."

"But I don't need to hide," the sting-ray tells her.

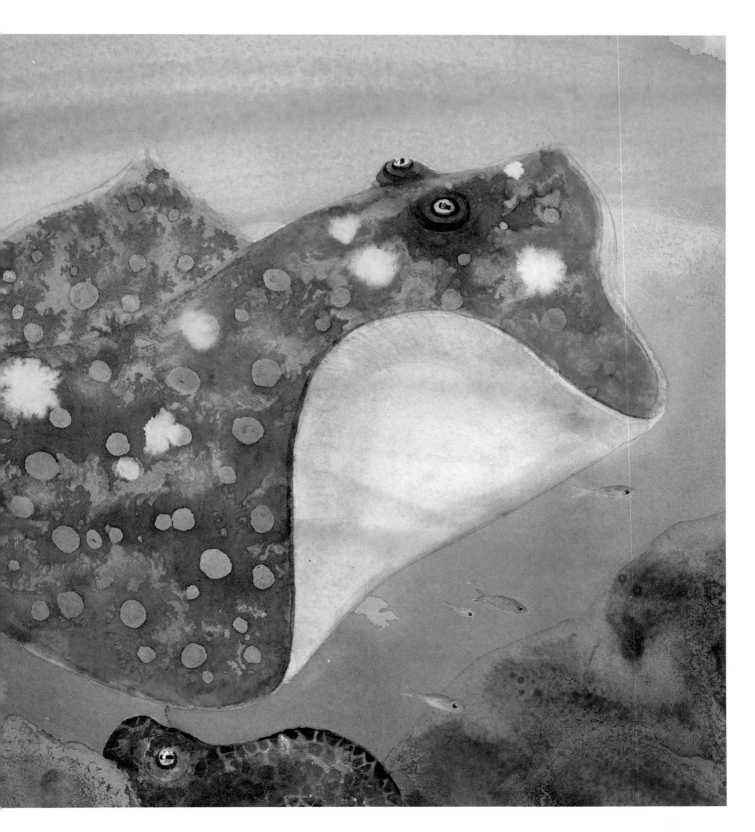

"I've a sting in my tail and I'll sting anything that comes too close!"

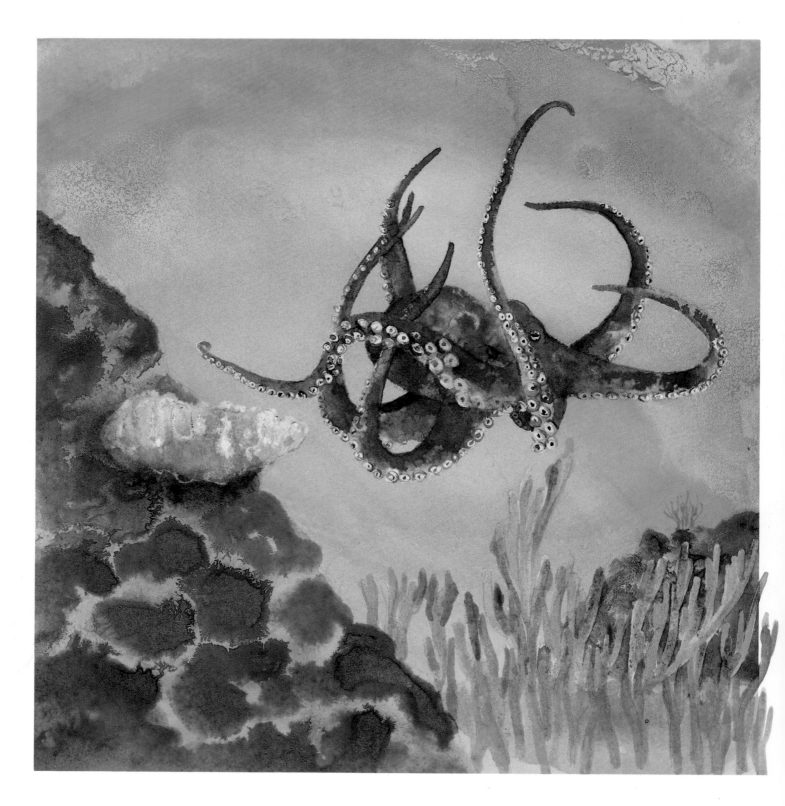

The octopus swims down to the bottom of the sea,
where she disturbs some weeds.

Out floats the leafy sea dragon, delicate and frail.
"Don't stay here," the octopus says, "there's something
trying to catch us."

So the leafy sea dragon drifts back into the weeds,

where it looks just like leaves.

The octopus swims on and the coral cod skims past,
glistening and bright.

"It's dangerous here!" the octopus says.
"You're much too easy to see."

"But nothing can see me when I hide,"
the coral cod tells her,

as it slips under a ledge and disappears.

Now the octopus propels herself up and passes a puffer fish, hovering and hanging quite still in the water.

"You must move!" the octopus says. "Something's coming after me and it will get you, too."

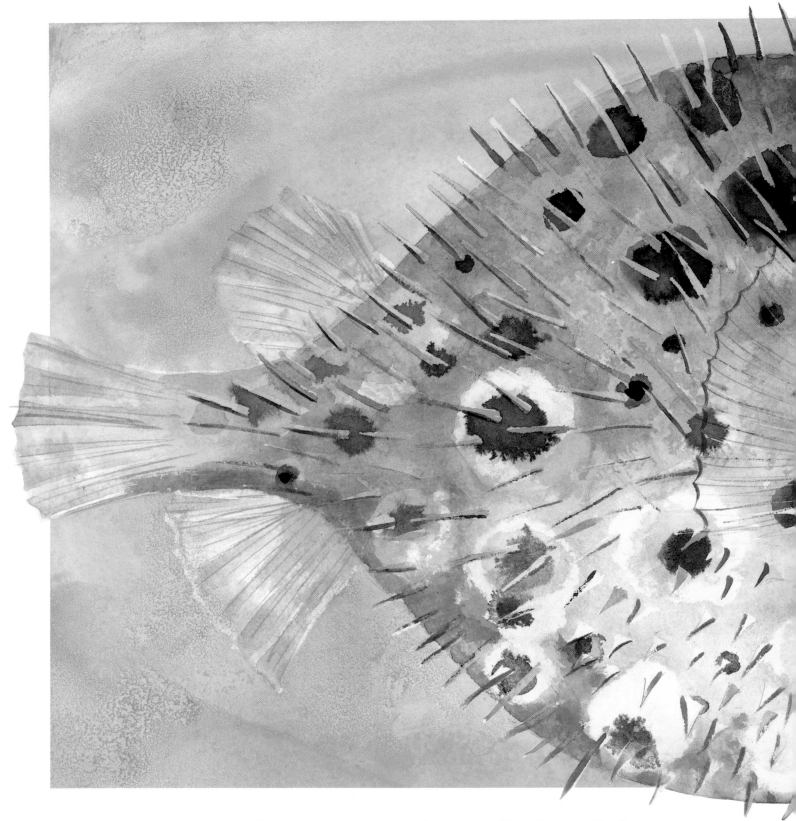

"Then I'll puff myself up," the puffer fish tells her.

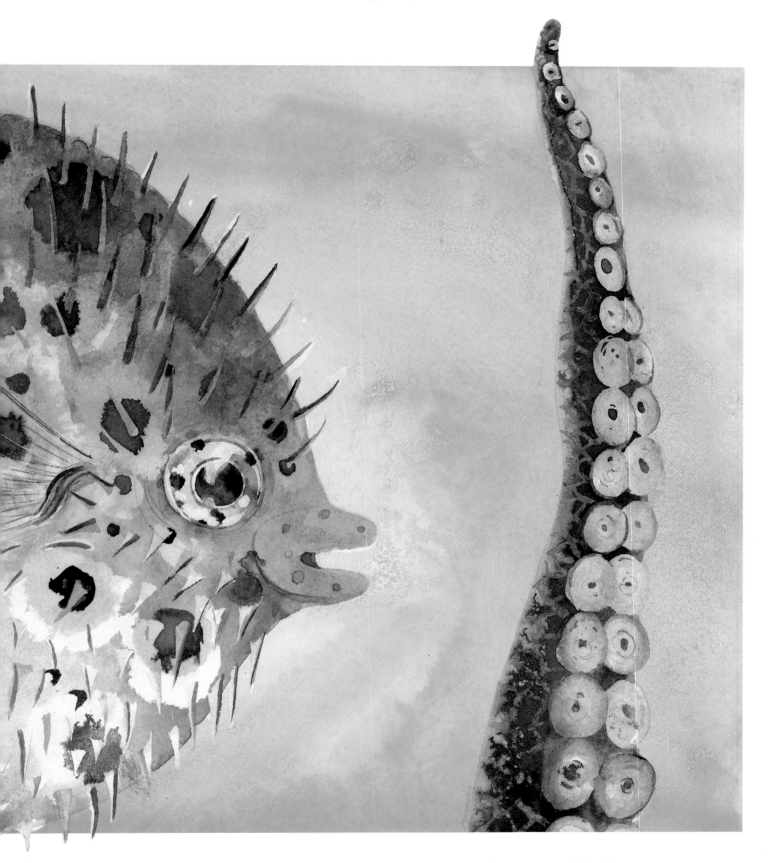

"I'll puff myself up like this, into a spiky round ball,
so that nothing can get hold of me."

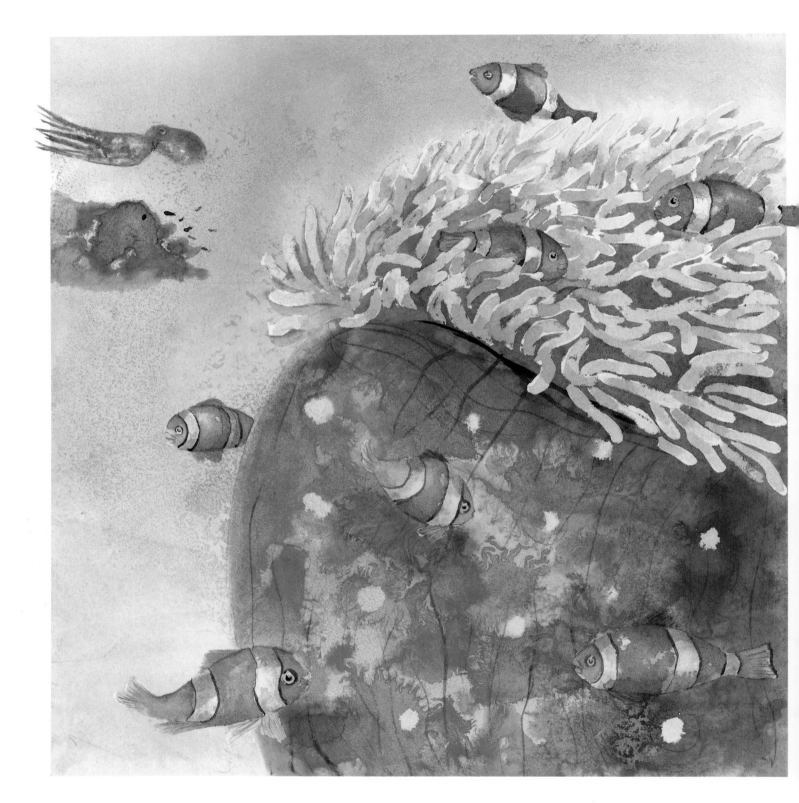

The octopus swims on and sees some small striped
clown fish clustering around the sea anemones.

"Quick, take cover," the octopus says.
"Something's on its way to get us."

"Then we'll hide right here inside the anemones," they tell her.

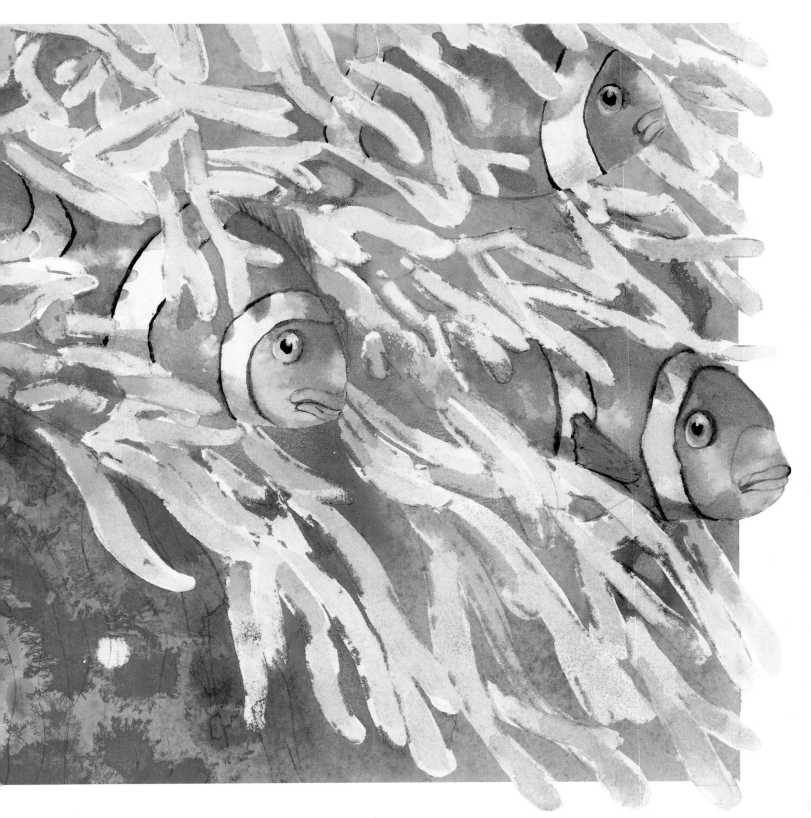

"But we're the only ones who can. The anemones are poisonous to other fish!"

The octopus swims on. She's nearly back at her den now.
She glides past some rocks, then stops with a shock.

Because the moray eel, wrinkled and grey,
is already there, waiting to pounce!

The octopus stares...

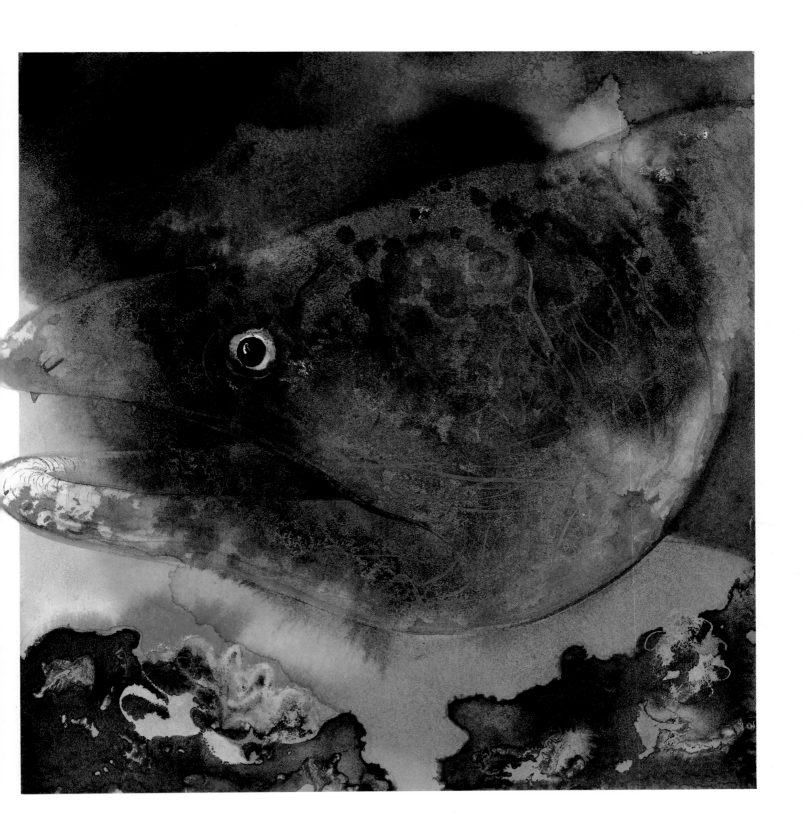

and suddenly squirts ink!

Now the water's so murky that the moray eel can't find her,

and the octopus finally reaches her den,

where she can be alone and safe at last.

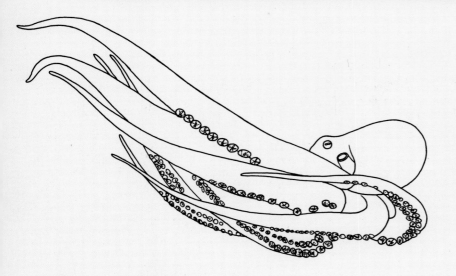

OCTOPUS

Some types of octopus are as small as a human finger while others grow to be the size of a small boat. This shy creature lives alone on the sea bed, often hiding in its den. When threatened it changes its colour, squeezing its body through tiny holes and cracks or squirting a cloud of ink to confuse its enemy.

STING-RAY

Flapping its body just like a large underwater bird, this flat fish moves gracefully through the waters of the reef. The sting-ray in this story would measure about 75cm from tip to tail and, when threatened by predators, it would use the sting in its tail to protect itself.

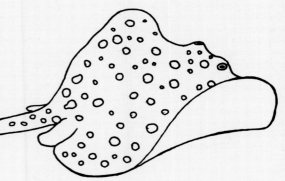

LEAFY SEA DRAGON

This strange creature carries its babies in a pouch, as a kangaroo would do. A type of sea-horse, it grows to about 30cm in length. Its leafy body looks like the twisting, floating seaweed of the reef, and so it hides itself among the weeds when it wants to avoid being seen by other fish.

CORAL COD

This is one of the most brightly coloured fish in the reef. It is about half a metre in length and manages to use the ledges, holes and crannies in the coral to hide itself away when there is danger.

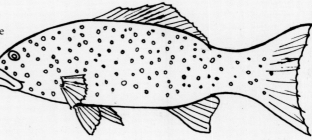

PUFFER FISH

When the puffer fish is threatened it sucks in water so that its body puffs out like a balloon, making it appear up to twice its usual size (normally 25–30cm). Some puffer fish also have sharp spines on their bodies, which stick out when they puff themselves up – too nasty a mouthful for most hunters.

MORAY EEL

This is the great hunter of the coral reef. In the open sea it can grow to 3m in length but on the reef it is usually about half this size. It hides its long body in the cracks and crannies of underwater caves, waiting to pounce on its prey.

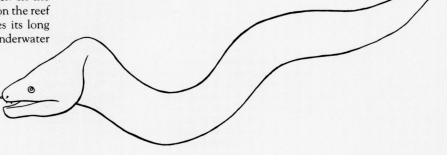

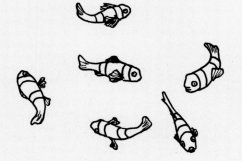

CLOWN FISH

Many fish live together and help each other. Brightly coloured clown fish live among poisonous anemones that shelter them. Their bright colours probably warn off enemies.

THE CORAL REEF

The coral reef is a vast living limestone structure created from the skeletons of tiny sea animals or polyps. These polyps live in shallow, clear, sunny patches of sea feeding on small creatures called plankton and, when they die, their bodies become part of the reef. Coral reefs are the largest constructions on earth to have been produced by living creatures and they can take thousands of years to grow. The Great Barrier Reef is the largest reef in the world and lies off the NE coast of Australia. This reef provides hiding places and homes for many different sea creatures, all of whom have a special way of escaping the hunters who search for them in their coral home. The Great Barrier Reef is the setting for this story.

First published in Great Britain, in Gollancz Children's Paperbacks 1995, by Victor Gollancz, a Division of the Cassell group, Villiers House, 41/47 Strand, London WC2N 5JE. Text copyright © Sue Vyner 1995. Illustrations copyright © Tim Vyner 1995. The right of Sue Vyner and Tim Vyner to be identified as authors of this work has been asserted by them in accordance with the Copyright, Designs and Patents Act, 1988. A catalogue record for this book is available from the British Library. ISBN 0 575 05935 4

Printed in China